I0579160

Love
Light & Dark

Kully Patel

Silver Grove Publications, LLC

ISBN-13: 978-1-948869-02-7

LOVE: LIGHT & DARK

Author: Kully Patel
Publisher: Silver Grove Publications, LLC

www.silvergrovepublications.com

This book is a work of fiction. Any references to realistic historical events, legends, myths, religions, items, and physical locations are used in a fictitious manner. All other locations, events, people, etc. are the product of the author's imagination; any resemblance to actual events, locations, or people – both living and dead – are coincidental.

This author is part of the Silver Grove Publications (SGP) family. If you have any questions or wish to browse our other SGP authors, please visit our website for books, products, and submission guidelines.

www.silvergrovepublications.com

CONTENTS

DEDICATION

Paul Marrero Jr.
(1955-2017)

My candle on the water.

PASSION
&
YOUTH

The Snowdrop blooms
Against icy green leaves
Bringing hope of Spring.

Love Me

Reach out your hand
And love me dear.
Hold me near
And always be here.

I need you always.
More today,
Less tomorrow.
It will always be there.

Listen to me,
The words are key.
Love me dear.
And be with me
— for eternity.

I Call Your Name

The quiet pitter of rain,
The steady beat,
Relaxes and soothes,
Smoothing all the pain away.

The sudden rocking,
Thunder crashes down,
I call your name,
Crawl deeper into bed
Hoping you will hear.

Flash of light,
Form in the window.
I call your name
Thunder crashes down.

Hands hold me.
I call your name.
A voice responds,
I am here.

All is quiet,
Storm has passed.
All is well,
You are here.

Kisses

Kisses, cool and passionate,
Dress my naked body
Like dew on a rose
On a warm summer morning.

Kisses, warm and wet,
Touch my hidden core
With a tongue of flame
Searching my soul
Quenching my thirst.

Kisses, soft and gentle,
Smother my body
As the first tendrils of sleep
Woo me into darkness.

Love Lasts Forever if...

Love lasts forever in reality
Yet happiness is a struggle
And the battle is worth the fight.

Happily ever after does not exist
And tomorrow problems will arise,
But tonight we shall lie in loving bliss.
The soft voice may be hard
In the argument which may come,
But the love does exist in the other's touch.

Gentleness hidden in hardness and pain
And the rain may seem to last,
But the love that is forever remains
In spite of hard words and blows.

The love that lasts forever
Dresses not in roses and dates,
But in dandelions and thistles
With chocolate for sweetness.

Scrapes and bruises matter not
In an everlasting love.
Only the other's joy and happiness matter
And trust remains on shattered ground
Like a beacon in the night.

Time Locked in a Bottle

Time locked in a bottle,
No way to release it.
Paper colored with ink,
No way to erase it.
Perfection you seek,
Impossible to get.
Player's passion,
The game just starts.
No chemical reaction
Can be love's reason.
The meeting of eyes,
The touch of a hand,
Tomorrow you seek,
Forever is banned.
Nothing makes sense
But boredom or sin.

Daydream

A quiet voice cheers me
Through a hard day
Like a ray of sunshine
On a stormy shore.
With every caressing note,
The ripples spark hope.
A mini-vacation,
An island oasis,
A fantasy interlude.
Reality doesn't intrude
As a quiet voice cheers me
Through a hard day.

16

Impatient longing
First blossom of youth
Time for love
Time for crying
Too tight shoes
Not enough money
Dreams abound
Straps sliding down
Camera clicks
Wine wet lips
Invitation to kiss
Two bodies greet
In nature's heat
A child too soon
An Adult too young.

Who to Choose?

My dreams unfold fickle
Like the warnings from above.
One loves me unconditionally,
One desires me passionately,
And one eyes me jealously.
Time to decide,
Time to choose.
Whose words woo me?
Whose heart do I trust?
Sadly, none today
As I learn to be me.

Never Regret

Never regret love, my dear.
The price may be high,
And very dear.
But the love given purely
Will be returned surely.
Maybe not as you think
But as you are blessed
With sudden kindness,
A forgiveness from the past,
Or a compliment unexpected.

Never regret love, my dear.
The pain may be devastating.
The agony never ending,
When love is not returned
Or used for purposes surreal.
But love given truly
Will bring forth healing.
The scars remain
As badges for memories sake.

Never regret love, my dear.
Only the bold understand
That unconditional love
Will heal our broken land.

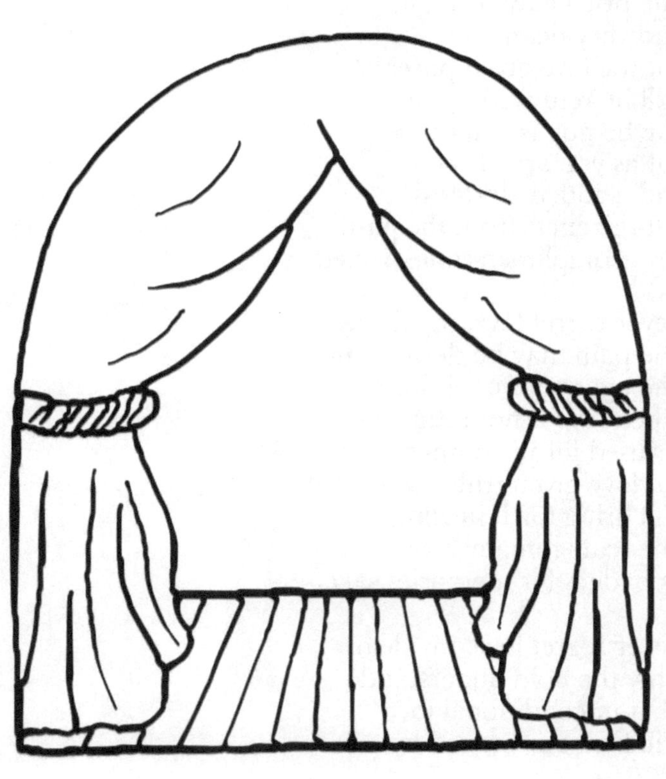

Alex MacGregor

And never, love,
Leave me crying
'Cept when you leave me, dying.

Make no promises,
Always tell me
The truth untold.
Give me your heart
Rough and torn.
Let me return
A heart and soul,
Right or wrong.

About This Poem:

In college, Kully had a boyfriend who played as this character. This poem is a reflection of the character and the story involved, as well as her connection to it.

Paths Interwoven

Our paths interwoven
Together with gentleness
That only true hearts can weave.
Our paths part and cross
With the regularity
Of birds flying South.
Our friendship follows the only path
Open to the pure heart.

My life complex, yours twisted;
Yet we meet again and again
As we follow the described path.
Laughter and tears litter the mood
With many, many years to brood.

Remember dear heart only we
Make the stretches apart pleasurable
So drink wine with friends
And return home to grow
Knowing our paths are interwoven.

The Electrons

Time past, Time present, Time to be.
Electrons fall into sequence.
Past to future does turn
As dreams of tomorrow are answered today.
One last chance for you and me
To recapture our glorious past
Which resounds through my room
With pictures of you.
Unicorn and bears to protect me
Keeps the memories alive.
The electrons scatter
Ripping us apart.
The electrons align,
Joining our hearts.

The Virgin

The gentle drawing of passion, so fierce.
The heat, so great.
The pain, so vivid,
And yet, so pleasant.
An urgent need, so undeniable.

The glorious awakening,
A slow burning flame.
Pain passes slowly,
Replaced by sweetness.
The body split,
Emotions churned.

A gentle caress
Soothes the pain away.
Kisses softly given,
A murmur heard
"I'm sorry. I love you."

Heat rises quickly.
Passion dawns stronger
Body arches seeking
Fulfillment of an ache.

Time's Interlude

The touch of a hand fires the soul
As passion rises and flames grow bold.
The caress of a hand and the joining of minds,
One self remains as two bodies combine.
Time lies suspended, and minutes hours become.

Confusion lies buried
Under the touch of the hand.
As souls unite in a lover's kiss.
Time lies suspended, and minutes hours become.

An impatient soul awaits
The touch of a hand.
Thoughts swirl in a mind lost,
No truth was gained.
One self remains as two bodies mate.
Time lies suspended, and minutes hours become.

The Flame

There is darkness;
Blacker than the night,
More fearful than the truth.
I reach out and strike the match,
Which I hold tight as it lights.

Then there is a flame;
Comforting, flickering
Like the one inside me.

The one that glows
Brightly when you are near
And dims when you leave.

The one that draws you near
And watches you go as it dies.

The match flickers out.
Darkness returns.

I can relight the match,
I can relight the inner flame.

The match for comfort,
The flame for you,
What do I want to do?

The answer you know.

Love is Your Truth

Love the broken in your soul: the gaping holes, the
    empty areas.
Love the ugly parts: the parts you don't like, the parts
    that make you cringe.
Love the dark parts: where sadness lives and emotions
    roil.
Love the secret powerful ego: the kinky and the kooky
    hidden self..
Love every dark and broken bit of you:
                    That is your Truth.

Innocence

Gossamer wings and Fairy Tales,
Turtle doves and pretty girls
Dance on the walls like tiny dreams.
Children's eyes open wide
Waiting for the witch to arrive.
Quiet moments swinging under the apple tree
Disappear unnoticed by all.
Beehive and purple thistle,
Oblivion at last.
Cars and dates, coming home late
Such a short time does the innocence last.

Shorts

A collection of short poems about passion and youth.

Time spent in sleep is never wasted.
The soul is reborn.
The heart is healed.
Dreams echo truth.
Hopes are born anew.
The body and heart sync.
Life begins anew.

The nectar of gods
Fills man's soul with soft sweetness
Defiled by man's sins.

The silence of night
Creeps through the earth's shadow
With a lover's stealth.

Glowing Red Embers
Burn Not in Purgatory
My soul writhes in pain
Without your hot flames.

On Mt Olympus
Venus drinks sweetened nectar
With truth absolute.

Moment of Silence
Fills the heart with quiet peace
And the eyes of beauty.

HEARTACHE
&
HEARTBREAK

Floating butterflies on pressed trees
Dancing here, stopping there.
Light's fire burns low
And the flames cease to glow.

Your Journey Begins

Seek the unknown in your soul
For there your journey begins.
Depend not on me to lead
For our paths only mingle.

My sight is yours for an asking
So travel with care and beware
The journey leads not out
But into your quivering soul.

Seek the unknown in your soul
For there, your journey begins.
Fear not the wandering path
Meander along my friend.

Your heart is your hidden guide
So trample with emotions
Lingering on as you go
Through your memories.

Seek the unknown in your soul
For there your journey begins.
In the end your heart will mend
And love will live ever more.

Desire's Seasons

The leaves have changed once more
And the year a complete round has turned.
We stand now where we were before,
Friends of a dubious nature with the need to touch.

Our eyes do not meet across the table
As they have so many times before,
But our trust has grown and wisdom blossomed.
Like children playing hide and seek, I search for you
In the early morning light to find answers among the
    new growth.

Oft I wonder if life would be better if we met never
And let what feeling is left die as friendship fades.
Yet when we meet, your face so dark touches my soul.
With your eyes that lie like dull coals
I feel a tug to stay and talk about your life.

How can you make some things right
When desire for your happiness keeps me here.
The leaves are all gone now
And winter's ice will soon fall.

Confusion blossoms into growth,
Understanding to hope,
Yet the pain remains to be felt.
Reach out your hand and grab mine
Never alone to be.

Joy

Joy escapes the divine chest last,
As Pandora slowly closes the lid.

Slow to escape, slow to come,
Joy seldom welcomes company.

Faith and Hope dance around like devoted dogs.

But, Joy rarely greets us at all.

Actions Not Taken

Paperwork received.
Reviewed and edited.
Only the silence remains.
A marriage asunder
Due to words not spoken,
Actions not taken,
And love forsaken.
Adultery starts in the head,
Ends in a bed.
Permission to withdraw requested.
Only memories remain,
And hopes of what might have been,
If words had been gentle and
Actions taken.

Frenemies

Are we friends?
We can talk.
We can love.
We can hate and desire.

Separate from each other,
Come back together.

Hold each other,
Hurt each other,
Make pain almost tangible
With words and bodies.

And yet…
As you walk out the door
I know
You will be back.

Sooner or later,
More likely later,
But return you will
And welcome I shall.

With open arms and heart
Always waiting for you
Through the same door.
The one you know so well.

Waiting for you to say,
Words or actions to speak
"I am back."

Are we friends?
I don't know.
I like to think so.
But who can tell?

We hide so well
Behind our masks.

Letting each other see
Only what we want to see.
Not showing our feelings
With words or movements.

So are we friends?
Yes, we are.
But not as close as should be.

Do You Remember

Do you remember
The tears we cried
On the day
You came to say
Goodbye?

It was a fine day
So like today
When you came to say
Goodbye.

The wind had blown
The cobwebs away
On the day
You came to say
Goodbye.

The birds sang sweet
Through the street
On the day
You came to say
Goodbye.

Unaware and unknowing
A kiss so sweet.
On the day
You came to say
Goodbye.

Only the Shell Remains

My heart is empty;
My soul has departed.
Only the shell remains.

The whisper of your name;
The sound of your voice;
An echo of what once was.

Only I stand alone
Without and barren.
No magic stayed.

Why did you leave?
Why did you have to go?
Why leave me alone?

My heart is empty;
My soul has departed.
Only the shell remains.

Divorce

The days are colder now
And the nights longer somehow
But the joy in my heart warms me
Like a cognac in the evening.
No more fighting,
No more harsh words,
No husband to support.
Only the silence of my thoughts
And the joy that fills my heart.

Emptiness

For the lack of communication,
For the lack of understanding,
For the lack of being…
All is empty.

Yet I feel haunted.
His name appears everywhere:
On cars, in files, in media,
Yet it is nowhere.

"He will be back," my friends say,
but I think "No chance."
The last dance has been played.

No looking back,
Running in opposite directions.
Truth unexpected nor liked.

He wanted to play,
But the rut was the same,
Just a different day.

"Trying to change," he says,
But to what avail?
Certain mannerisms are deep,
Patterns play out.

Once I wished for him.
Now I pray for him
To have the life he chooses
As he hides in his cave.

All is empty
When only the past remains.
The rest is just empty
When dreams haunt the day.

Fight We Must

Why, my love, do we fight?
Why, my love, can we not like?
Needing you as I do,
Why must venom our words make?
Desire flames high
As Passion answers swift.
Yet words of anger emerge
From innocent thoughts spoken.
Trust remains broken.

Marriage

Time shifts with every season,
Words with no meaning bond us
In useless matrimony.
Betrayal on both sides.
Communication lost in pain,
Let us not hurt each other
With angry words or flaying fists.
Freedom I seek to end the pain,
No more days of wondering if you will speak,
No more listening to your tired voice
Telling me how dumb I am.
Just sweet freedom to sit and be.

My Love, My Life

Happiness flits in.
Happiness flits out.
Wisdom and hope guide
Impatient hearts
And misguided passion
To journey's end.

Good-bye, my love.
Hello, my love.
Time churns thru life
As seasons change.

My heart leads me on
An adventurous road.
Growth and pain,
Sorrow and shame,
Happiness comes again.

The past repeats
Until I decide to let go.
Forever the same
Yet never the same.
Someday I will love
As I did with my hero.
My strength and my rock
Too soon gone.
My love ever lasting
Yet I try to replace my loss.

All else pales.
My soul mate raises my passion,
His heart I hear,
His emotions I feel.
But my soul mate I cut free,
For he is not for me.
He is not my rock
Nor my hero.
His lies a constant,
His choices a sham
At love he plays.
I release him with my blessing
I release him with forgiveness
I release him so I can choose me.
Happy I will be.

Period

Moments pass
In dark solitude.
Alone I sit
Awaiting release
From depression's dark hand.

Pain wells up
Engulfing my soul
And a tear of blood flows
Into my tender core.

When will my savior come,
Where will we meet?
The pain steadily grows.
Tears form not,
Only those of blood exist.

Love's gentle hands penetrate not
To the tender core being torn
By depression's dark hand.
Only the pain remains as
The tears of blood flow

Where Lies Claim the Day

Your dark eyes leave me naked.
A single glance and my soul is revealed.
No lies can remain.
No hope can stay,
As passion rules the day.
Fear and lust vie
As our bodies collide.
Tingling and burning
Souls joining.

Your dark eyes leave me naked.
A single glance and my soul is severed.
Your words were lies,
Fear presided where truth resided.
Can love remain where lies claim the day?
Fear of loss caused untruths to fall.
A baby conceived with another's egg
As your thoughts were of me you say.

Your dark eyes leave me naked.
Your return, your sojourn into the cave of truths.
Me you need for happiness to be.
Yet can love remain where lies claim the day?
Truth most stark reveals the dark
A Dad you will be.

Guilt and remorse die
Under forgiveness's eye.
Yet can love remain where lies claim the day?
Trust lay broken,
Passion remains.
Your dark eyes leave me naked.

Memories

Memories tucked away
Upstairs in an old chest
Of the times we spent
Together.

Pictures and old love letters
Make the tears fall slowly.
Was it me?

Holding hands,
Days spent in the sun.
Now it's gone.
Chest is shut.
The memories tucked away…
Again.

Only the Silence Remains

Only the silence remains
The voices of loved ones are gone,
Distant echoes of what once were faded,
The glow of Joy departed 'till
Only the silence remains.

No evening songs or gay repartee,
Sparkling wines flow no more,
Parties have passed the midnight hours 'till
Only the silence remains.

Trusted confidences are broken.
A shattered soul cried helplessly,
Piteously, 'till
Only the silence remains.

The unsaid words regretted no more.
The love unnurtured has died.
The silence floods in 'till
Only the silence remains.

Empty Nest

Her room is empty now,
Dolls are all gone,
Not even her books remain.
The silence sends me running
To see what she is doing.
I catch myself calling her name.
Yet I know I will see her again.
Will this day never end?

The phone rings,
"Yes Mom, It's me." She says;
I breathe a sigh of relief.
Maybe college isn't so far away.
Maybe my girl is still near.

Do You Think of Me?

Saw your picture on the Internet yesterday.
Looking at you I saw the past
and wondered
        If you still think of me

Grown now you are yet still the same
Your face, your hair, your eyes look older
and yet I wonder
        If you still think of me.

The times at the beach, the times at home
Never alone and yet always just us.
A love never quite requited
and yet always there
        If you still think of me.

Twisted Lips

Words fall from twisted lips
As power gently changes hands.
Innocence presumed, quickly betrayed
At politician's hands.
Bodies meet in secret rooms
To be cold once again in public politics.
All the games being played
Men keep score in dollars and pain.
Women watch and plot for the day
When they will reign.

Mistake

So you think you made a mistake?
Everyone makes them,
Very few admit them,
No one likes them.

But you think you made a mistake?
What could you have done,
Why won't you tell,
Are you afraid or simply don't care?

So you made a mistake? Big deal!
Everyone does.
But the bigger mistake --
Telling it all over town

So yeah, you did.
You made a mistake.
You opened your mouth.
The words poured out,
Truth and Lies intertwined.

Gossip and rumors fly.
The mistake becomes lost
Within the legend.
So yeah,
      you made a mistake.

Tohubohu

A state of utter confusion
As the past and present collide.
Tohubohu —
Two souls re-engage as if tomorrow was yesterday.
Spouses cast aside
Passion collides on a bed far away.
Tohubohu —
A state of utter confusion
Emptiness and truth
Love destroyed and renewed.
Tohubohu —
A state of utter confusion remains
As lies pave the way
For secret meetings near and far
Bringing sin to the floor.
Tohubohu —
A state of utter confusion

Wishes

Quiet wishes cast
Amongst a turbulent sea.
I wished,
I dreamed
Of you and me.

Fireplaces, warm and soft,
Hot chocolate, sweet and rich,
Throw pillows, large and comfy,
And you with me, tender and loving.

The sea carried you off today
So far away.
Only quiet wishes remain.

Waiting

Time passes slowly while I wait for you.
I wonder if you miss me too.
Our moment together a forgotten lie,
Or enshrined and heart-tied.
They await to revive
A love grown cold.
An ache remains soul-bound
Reminding me I had found
My other half in you.

Words

Your words hurt.
Your words heal.
Your words say "I love you"
Your actions hurt.
Your actions bring passion.
Your actions leave me
Without my heart's desire.

Alone but stronger and ready
For a forever happily ever after
I move forward without regret.

My words hurt you not.
My words spark desire.
My words say "You love me not"
My actions bring separation.
My actions bring forgiveness.
My actions say "I Love You"
Without breaking a connection.

Alone but stressed and confused
You stand bearing your responsibility.
You move forward into the unknown.

Love Left Behind

My life alters with the shifting sands of time.
Moving to and fro, my pendulum swings
Charging back and forth with the tides of life.

What transitional force pushes my life
Playing havoc with its balance,
Causing tears on my pillow
With each shift of emotion?

Love my dear.
Love you caused.
Love you left behind.

Shorts

A collection of short poems about heartache and heartbreak.

Separation comes
From the parting of two hearts
Not from the distance of two people.

Understanding comes
From time spent apart in peace
The mood has moved on
To happiness and so
Life rules, not darkness.

Love's glorious face
Draws beauty on ugliness
And hope on sin.

The pain of loving
A bittersweet beauty of
Great pleasure and joy.

In the dark soil
I plant Passion Flower seeds
To heal my heartbreak.

White paper
Random thoughts
Closing doors
Opening hearts

LOSS & DEATH

Mendenhall Glacier
Destroys history and time
As daily melt flows.

A Life Asunder

A torn piece of lace,
A picture bent with age,
A life torn asunder
All that remains of a soul.

The will of God has spoken,
Sentencing just and true.
The path to tread alone
Until the fire of the night calls you.

No glory to be found
As the battle ground lay buried
'Neath the heart broken.

No hope to preserve
In the soul broken.
Friends long gone
Drift by to say
Good-bye.

Dad

In the silence of my heart,
My tears fall without recall.
Memories of you fill my mind.
The hurt that remains binds
The brokenness of my heart.

Your ashes scatter,
The waves crash,
One last goodbye.

Dearest Heart

Love blossoms and dies;
Causes unknown.
The promises remain,
Free and untouched.
Remember my heart,
Forget me not.
Elders regret
Their sins of youth.
Love, hindered,
Averted and blocked,
Slowly fades away.
Time's cruel hands,
Fades the memory
Of most passions
From your mind.
Remember me, my love
For again we shall meet.

Death

The winds upon us downward fall
As darkness and light do wed.
Our death,
A simple snip of the thread,
Our life cannot forestall.
Venture out not this night
Friends linger by the door.

Our hearth serves as a reminder
Every stone a memory of
Drunken euphoria or somber death
Dancing the sweet eternal life.

The morning light casts a shadow
On mourners gathered round.
The casket lowered to the ground.
Sadness, confusion, and a piano,
Friends linger in the church.

Never again a morn to see
As change will never be.
Our death, our life cannot stop.
Woe unto me.

Depression

Flames leaping, licking and lapping
At the burning pages of my mind.
Eating through my conscious
All the way to my heart.
Pain etching lines
Through my unawareness,
Futilely trying to awaken my soul.
Oh, blessed fire rescue me.
Remove from me my heart.
Take me to blessed darkness
For the rest of my days.

Dying

Emotions float through brittle ways
As shattered thoughts encase broken hearts.
Fluttering birds and singing bees dance
On icy lakes.
Only silence screams over the memories.
Glory begins and ends in death.
Dancing gives into rituals
As the end draws near.

Foi

Unto these perishable bodies we are born,
The soul that lights us afire we adorn
With the glory of our acts and our selfless wisdom.
Upon our final OM, we depart this earthly kingdom
To sojourn onto a heavenly place
Where indestructible we face
The impenetrable truth of us:
All that are born, die
All that die are born.
So grieve not with tears of sadness,
Grieve with the joys of my life.
I who loved you so
Now rest upon a bed of snow.
My soul has gone to a new home
Where I await you once more.

Lonely Heart

Rivers flow past
Leaving me behind.
Sitting alone
On the desolate shore,
Wishing I could follow
The roaring water.

My heart cries out
To the emptiness.
Darkness surrounds
My deserted world.
A heavy stone lands
On my sore heart.

Tears form in my grey eyes,
Falling down my cold cheeks.
Nothing penetrates
The walls of loneliness erected tall.

Walking through the empty world,
I see nothing, no one.
Feeling my way, blindly.
Emptiness surrounds me.

Opening to the world,
Pain floods in.
I cannot stand.
My body lies weakened and lonely.
I fade into the black river.

Love Birds

The love birds coo in the trees
Free and happy like the bees.
He dances in the sky,
She watches him dive by.
Cheep, coo, cheep, coo
Love birds pass the day.

A serpent slides in
To flirt and play.
She tries to soar away
But foreign grasp
Holds her fast.

He swoops down
In an angry dance,
Kills her
In a lover's spat.
The serpent swells
And swallows whole
Two love birds for his repast.

The Picture

A lace fan broken carefully held.
Once belonging to a creased face,
Drawn against a soft background,
Etched with memories from yesterday.
Green-grey eyes faded,
Hair once black
Ivory skin and
Jaded expression.
Laughter lost,
Hidden by a mirror.
Quiet stateliness
Roars within a
Softly falling tear.

Rejoice, My Love

Listen, my love, to the cries of the birds
In the fading daylight they sing.
The sun slips from the sky
As the life slips from his lips.

Be not sad for he has left
For a better shore to be found.
The pain in life is his no more.
Rejoice for his happiness now.

Be not sad, my love.
His departure was painless.
Rejoice for a better world he has found.

Rejoice, my love, be not sad.

Death Comes as an End

Death comes as an end, they say.
Yet life is a little death each day.
Coffee cups filled with cream
Swirl with energetic dreams.
Universes spiral in each sip
As imagination begins to dip
Into realms of stars shining bright.

One Autumn Day

Dried flowers blowing across the walk,
Dead leaves rambling by the road,
Paper pieces float on by,
Alone with wandering thoughts sit I.

No one is near,
No one is dear.
Trust lies dead,
Friends walk away.
Winter's chill awakens my soul.

Blue Roses

Gather blue roses while you can
For tomorrow the acid rain may fall
And burn into our fried tennis shoes
To bring our minds back to bombs
Set off in the middle of a SNAFU
By men who carry poached pencils now.

Gather blue roses while you can
And sit upon Elephant Rocks
Discussing the holocaust
Created by the nuclear bombs.

With a mensch who says,
"The end is the end;
Nothing remains but
Hollow corpses and empty bones.
There is no Heaven and no Hell.
Escape is death and death – the end,
Your impending doom."

Gather blue roses while you can
Virgins and sinners alike.
The mensch said the end is the end
And I say there will be more.
So enjoy what time of left
Until the bombs rain down again.

Remains

As wisdom floats out the door,
The mind forgets with age.
My heart remembers
Our last embrace.

Tears pour down
My wrinkled face
As loneliness descends.
Your eternal sleep,
My quiet slumber.
I miss your voice
As walls close in.

I scream your name
But only the memories remain.

Black Angels

The blue dawn greets
The bloody earth
On the eighth day
Of the last month
Of our final year.
The half alive lay
Groaning in the morn,
While the seekers return.
Angelic in form,
Black armor gleaming,
Firing aimlessly at the still earth.

An occasional scream
A brief flaring of light.

These dark angels of mercy
Come floating down from above
To land on the scorched earth,
Seeking survivors of a failed creation.

Terminate, Terminate, Terminate
Resounds through their minds.
Slowly the screams are gone.
Angelic in form,
Black armor gleaming,
Slowly floating away for no life remains.

Black Angels Return

The day blows in,
Cold and dreary
As flames die down,
The Angels of Black
Appear once more.
Their shiny weapons glow
In the meek morning sun.
Their work never done,
Their search, never-ending.
They pause,
Spotting something,
They fire in turn.
All is done.
Once again the world has ended,
And all is dead.

Listen

Listen!
Silence,
Not a sound.
Quiet,
Peace after so many years.

Withdraw!
Get away.
Troops march home;
No wars will be won or lost today.

Robots remain where no one can be found.
Pushing buttons,
Setting off bombs,
The only survivors in a children's game.

Listen!
Silence,
Not a sound.

A Dancer's Parting

With dancing feet and a joyous smile
Every day a new adventure,
I leave you sadly on my journey
To the heavens above.

My wit and my humor remember please.
My shoes and hats keep near.
But most of all my love and affection
For all I hold dear remains as I
Drift into my eternal rest.

Reverie

Sweet memories of days long gone,
Gently dancing throughout my mind.
A quiet daydream filled with joyous thoughts.
A voice breaks through,
Dreams evaporate into dew.

Ennui

Lingering laughter echoes back
Like the memories of the past.
Vague visions of what was and wasn't
Dance like Damocles' sword above.
Unrest fills the world, shattering
The ennui that passes as life.
Difference highlighted as an excuse
For a war to dispel the emptiness.

The Beach

One soldier sits on the beach.
Alone with no one watching his back.
Comrades lost to snipers' bullets.
Snipers lost to his.

One soldier sits on the beach.
Stars twinkle in the night's sky.
Red blasts continue behind him,
As rockets drop from the sky.

Three soldiers approach the beach,
Stealthy they come in a jeep.
Rendezvous point in sight.
Urgently, ready to escape.

Three soldiers reach the beach,
Silently they greet.
Four soldiers leave behind
The demise of a land full of hate.

Home again, safe on the compound.
Mourning the loss of friends.
Beer and tears flow equally
As the success is claimed
By Anchors who do not know
The loss felt in each heart.

The Capitol Burns

Chilling scenes
Mobs swarm
As hate becomes the norm.

Tears shed
More dead
Anger subsides
Confusion resides

A nation forlorn
Peace torn
Not to be reborn.

In the Name of Democracy

Rockets explode
Gun fire reports
Fights for freedom
In lands far away

Are we right
To use our might
To win their fights?

Voices echo
Tenseness reigns
Battles yet to be won
U.S. steps into the ring
On foreign soil
In the name of Democracy

Yet when freedom's won
Those who remain
Do not bless our name

Are we right
To use our might
To win their fights?

The Desk

Students sit on my endless gloss
Carving names into me.
Always dying, I never survive
Their need to destroy;
Soon the floor will remain,
Lights gone forever.
Slowly the paint crumbles
And I will be used for firewood.
Too abused to be sold,
Too used to recycle,
Sorry that the children are gone.
Flames dance on my varnish
as I collapse
and turn to ash.

Wisdom Instilled

The memories may blacken with age,
And the mementos lie broken and forgotten,
But the love and wisdom instilled
Burns on vividly forever.

The time for us to part has come,
You have gone.
The wisdom I seek is my own.
But I will forever draw on your strength,
Bound like a child to your love.

The Sky Weeps

Today, the sky weeps with me
As our adventures float through my mind
Like grains of sands falling
Through the hourglass of time.

Your smile never leaves me,
Your strength still supports me,
And your spirit sustains me
Even as my hands no longer find yours.

As your spirit roams
On an adventure alone now,
I mourn and weep.
Today, the sky weeps with me.

Death All Around

Death all around.
Encircling us into the ground.
Covid, a modern-day plague,
Violence, an everyday event,
Wars and famine abound.

Death all around.
My heart resounds.
Depression on every face
Grief in every place.

Death all around.
No peace is found.
As I look to the sky
Hope flies away.

Death all around.
Another soul rises
To the heavens.

Tombstone

I leave you here all alone
To sit and remember the gone.
Only death separates us now.
Only life keeps the vow.

Forever love,
Unconditional love.
Forever's kiss,
Tomorrow's bliss.

Lost and gone,
I leave you here,
all alone, my dear.

Final Words

The sun's final light
Draws the day to a close.
I have always watched it
From my window up here.
The slums of India encroach
Upon the apartments now.
No one's here,
But now you come Dear Doctor.
I sent them away,
So they would not see
My final breath,
And I would not see
The pointless tears drop
From their eyes and mine.
We have always known
That I would die soon.
I hope they know I loved them
And I will keep all the promises I made,
Especially about the weddings.
The harder I fought,
The shorter the time I had.
You said I couldn't walk,
I walked.
Everything seems so useless now
That it is almost over.
So once again I am at the edge
Between the beginning and ending.
Look, the sun has left and all is dark
These final moments are so precious.
I hope they understand why
And know how I felt.

The uselessness of wishing appears now,
Though hope remains to linger on.
Regrets have left me barren.
Oh, the pain.
Please give the letters
In my chest to them with love.
It hurts.
I wish it would leave.
I can't hang on.
Good-bye, my loves.

MOMENTS IN TIME

Pen across paper
No Cohesion
Only the confusion of blue on white.

Seasons

The laughing sweetness of Summer,
A dalliance in winter has begun.
The burning passion of Ice,
Confusion in Spring dissolves
Summer's sweetness melts
As Autumn's leaves Fall.

Tired Thoughts

Tired thoughts
Energy drained
Only hope remains

No future
No past
Nothing ever lasts

Just blurs
And twirls
And puppy dog curls

Tired thoughts
Random words
Only hope remains

Selenite

A crystal rod to cleanse,
A heart chakra's friend.
Random breaking,
Shattering,
Shattering,
Negative energy absorbed.
Emotional backlash sealed
Into the white congeal.
Released!
Each shard a healing fragment
For the heart.

The Portal

Open the door stands
Like a gate to the stars.
Beyond, darkness looms
Welcoming the dreams of night.
Tomorrow, emotions float through
Like pulses in the stars.
Beacons, words shining
Teem the entryway so far.
Slowly, steps taken
Through the hallowed gate.

Red Racer

Round and round the wheels roll,
Down and down the wagon goes.
Over the hill and past the pond,
Flying by in a blur of red.

The Rock Moves Slowly

The rock moves slowly
Yet it did move,
No longer firm or solid,
No longer protective.

The water rushes in
With confusion in its stead.
Faith becomes questioned,
How could you let this happen?

Memories stir of the past.
The rock moves again,
The water lies trapped,
Confusion remains,
But faith is restored.

Thoughts

Random ideas that wander across the blank page of my
   mind
Floating free yet interwoven and mingled like a windmill
Turning round and round, grinding and grinding
Drifting here and floating there
Hitting cement… splat!

No and yes, yes and no,
Over and over --- repeatedly.
Past and present, violet flowers,
Bittersweet regrets,
Yet no remorse.

Only the hoarse voice in my head
Brings peace, brings anxiety,
Harbinger of a restlessness to my soul.

What to write, what to do…
No forward, no back,
No truth, no lies,
Just thoughts
Going round and round.

Writer's Block

Words wrestle with thoughts
As ideas float by like tiny bubbles
From a children's pipe.

Chem II

Many moments I have spent
Sitting in Chemistry - sleeping.
Many hours I have used
Solving problems I understood.

I remember still the hours I sat
Listening to Mrs Mac chat.
I remember the awful smell
Of H2S diffusing the air.

The theories
      How Boring!
The problems
      My Poor Aching Head!
The titrations and laws
      Oh Please Stop!
The headaches and fun,
How I remember them well.
Just thinking of them I sleep swell.

Taj Mahal

Built out of love
To show its eternal power,
A palace of white stone
With gleaming towers
By a shining lake
Surrounded by greenery.

Shah Jahan for Mamtaz built
The gleaming tomb.
The mourning when she was gone
Turned the pristine tomb
Into a monument of eternal love.
With inlaid mosaics,
No replica allowed.

Power and pride befell him
As a black Taj Mahal
Was being created.
His son's command
Annihilated his breath,
So together buried
they remain.

An eternal love where grief
Turned the law into a tomb.

A King's Sin

The pain passes slowly
As sins of old are paid
By the price of a Kingdom lost
And a Queen's loving betrayal.
Arthur's sin stands
On the peak of double disaster.
A sister's evil deed,
Permanent downfall seeked.
Darkness falls over all,
Wisdom lost.
Heart's desire, dreams afire,
A King without a sword.
The chalice full of hope
Found in Mordred's evil grasp.
Morgain's spells and
Merlin's ghostly war.
An end so swift.
No clear King.
Confusion rules.
What was gained
In the end?

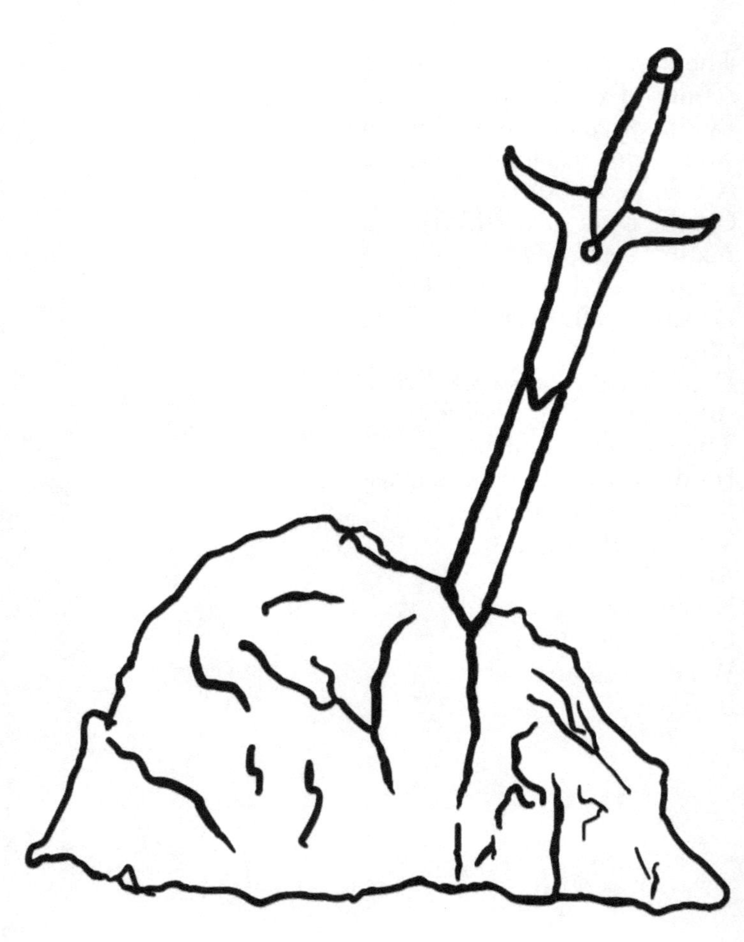

A Kingdom Regained

Roses blossom again
Guinevere appears.
Did he return?
Uther's son and heir.
Sin's instant comprehension
Forgiveness granted.
The might of the Brits
Rule the isle again.
United once more,
Arthur reigns strong
After the third war.
Hail Excalibur!

Picturesque

Waves lapping against an empty shore
With a continuous rhythm.
The grey sea calling
Home the ships long gone.
Sky filled with dark clouds
Announcing a storm approaching.
The lighthouse preparing
For a fog of pea soup.
The desolate beauty of the land
Striving to meet the restless shore.

Grassy plains rolling free
Meeting the blue sky
Near the edge of the world.
A horse free and untamed
Runs towards the nothingness
In majestic, unconscious beauty.
A heart string pulled,
Stirring for freedom and a desire to roam.

The red-streaked sky
Greets the sudden coming
A lone wagon across
A black barren plain.
Hate's cruel message
Destroys all
Except the lone wagon
Rolling across the black barren plain.

Blue sky of eternity draws the crawlers near
From their dark sky world.
Promise, hope, and fear
Countenance unrevealing
Grouping close they step
Into the forbidden world.
Discontent returns and beauty burns
And peace never remains.

Decadence

A mouth gently descends
Onto the rod, hot,
Speckled with coarse salts
And filled with white.
Slowly a bite is taken,
Enjoyed and loved.
Once again the mouth returns
To the pretzel.

Daybreak

Second by second
Bit by bit
Silently and quietly
Surely creeping
Over the mountain
Suddenly blooming

Light shines down
The world is silent
War has ended
The word rings out
The Lord has come

Writer's Lot

Words flow like a gentle breeze,
The kiss of a butterfly,
So smooth, so soft.
The day shines like a crystal palace,
The beauty ethereal and pure.
The whispers echo like a dream
As words continue to flow,
Violent and grinding
Pulling forth in a flurry of syllables.
Pen to paper,
Ink appears on the screen
As we search for the plot.

In the Arms of My Book

In the arms of my book
Every moment seems a little stranger,
The walls grasp out with hidden hands
As I rest in the arms of my book.

The flying dragons soar fearlessly.
The griffons threaten ferociously.
I grasp my sword and fight,
Nestled in the arms of my book.

The world turns upside down
As the evil sorcerer cast his spell,
I strike out trying to protect the princess
Snuggled in the arms of my book.

Like the Red Leaf

Changes take place all around
As Summer to Autumn bounds.
Like the red leaf floating in the stream,
I sail through storms my mind dreams.
The light of day pacifies not my fears,
Yet darkness holds them not near.
The night brings only dreams of peace
Without the need for release.
Mental mazes around my heart whirl
Guarding the way to my world.
Blue is not the color of my soul,
Grey in my life does not toil.
Red with passion and beauty dances
In the eternal vibrating prance
Through my world with slow steps of a dream
Like the red leaf floating in the stream.

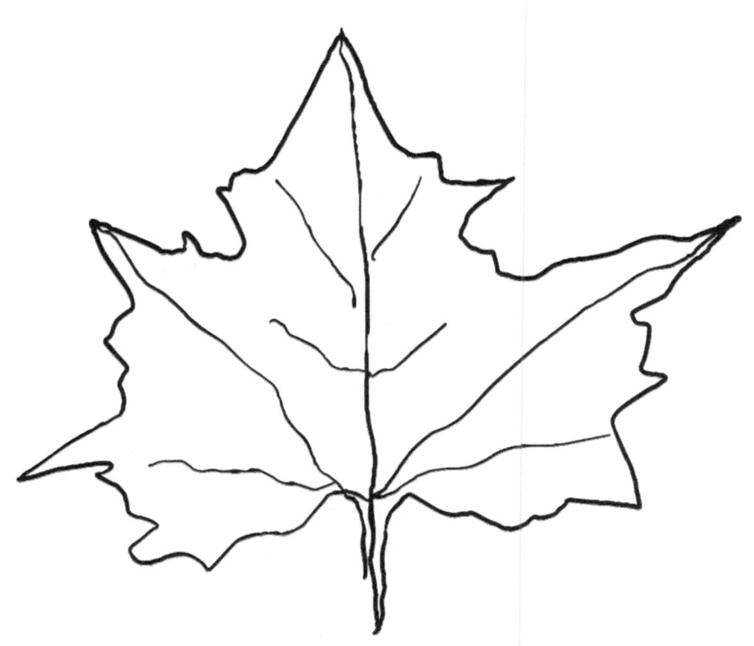

About the Author

A Life Lived Well has Love, Adventure, and Fun

Some lives are full of adventures, and Kully Patel's life is one of them. She was born in Bombay, India when it was still called Bombay, India. Her first airplane ride was when she was 2 years old when she moved to the USA with her family. With such an auspicious start, she has travelled the world in search of fun, experiences, and adventure. Her motto is "Sounds fun! Let's do it."

Kully Patel pours her emotions and empathy into her writing. They reflect who she is and what she feels. Due to her wide range of experiences in her life and her travels, her poems mirror her passion for beautiful things. Her descriptions give a glimpse into a moment in time.

Kully Patel started writing in high school. She explored short stories, technical papers, poems, haiku, and sonnets during her time in school and college. As she entered the working world, her love of poems solidified; she would jot down poems as gifts to friends and family. As she grew older, her poems reflected events throughout time and life that caught her attention.

As with any life, the older she got, the more often she was asked to write poems for funerals. To offset the grimness of death, Kully would also write a love poem so that the candle going out would also light the other candle called hope.

After the death of her father, Kully Patel found a box of her poems that her dad had saved. With some encouragement from friends and family, she decided it was time to publish her works. Every word in every poem reflects an unconditional love for everything, making life worth living.

Currently, Kully Patel is working on her writing and plans to publish more works in the future. She continues her adventuring and pouring her love for life and people into her writing.

Acknowledgements

I would like to thank Silver Grove Publications for making this dream a reality and walking with me on this path. Jennifer and the marketing team, thank you for the magic that you do. I would also like to thank Sandie and Michael for introducing me to the amazing founder of SGP, Maegan. She is truly a force.

Mom and Dad, I appreciate that you kept all my writings from when I was a teenager. Without your contribution, this book would never have come into being. I love you.

Thanks to Jeff Steward for inspiring me to write during college and supporting me through the development of this book. Your guidance has been invaluable to me. Also, thanks to James Shoemaker for having the patience to listen to me during the darkest times of my life and to Victor Allen Chapel Jr for inspiring several poems.

Also, this book is to my Paul. You took a broken and abused young girl and molded her into the woman I have become. Without you, my life would have lacked love, light, and adventure. I miss you every day. You continue to be my candle on the water, my rock and my strength.

Finally but never last, I want to thank Jennifer Key for all her support, love, and friendship through the years and my sister Mamta Kinsel without whom I would not have survived the death of our dad. Without both of you, I would be lost. I love you always.